THE WILY WOODCHUCKS

BY GEORGIA TRAVERS *author of "The Story of Kattor"*

ILLUSTRATED BY FLAVIA GÁG

MINNESOTA

Minneapolis University of Minnesota Press *London*

THE FESLER–LAMPERT MINNESOTA HERITAGE BOOK SERIES
This series reprints significant books that enhance our understanding and appreciation of Minnesota and the Upper Midwest. It is supported by the generous assistance of the John K. and Elsie Lampert Fesler Fund and the interest and contribution of Elizabeth P. Fesler and the late David R. Fesler.

To David Hedrich

Georgia Travers [Alma Schmidt Scott] (1892–1974) wrote numerous books for children, including *The Story of Kattor*, also illustrated by Flavia Gág. She was the childhood friend of Wanda Gág and the author of her biography, *Wanda Gág: The Story of an Artist*, published by the University of Minnesota Press in 1949.

Flavia Gág (1907–1979) was an author and illustrator of eight children's and young adult books. She was the younger sister of famed author and illustrator Wanda Gág.

First published in 1946 by Coward-McCann, Inc.
First University of Minnesota Press edition, 2009

Published by the University of Minnesota Press
111 Third Avenue South, Suite 290
Minneapolis, MN 55401-2520
http://www.upress.umn.edu

ISBN 978-0-8166-6548-8
A Cataloging-in-Publication record for this book is available from the Library of Congress.

Printed in the United States of America on acid-free paper

The University of Minnesota is an equal-opportunity educator and employer.

16 15 14 13 12 11 10 09 10 9 8 7 6 5 4 3 2 1

THE WILY WOODCHUCKS

TWO smug and contented woodchucks lived in a cozy hillside burrow in New Jersey. There were acres of sunny meadows in which they could amble about leisurely. There were smooth, flat rocks on which they could lie comfortably sunning themselves. And there were sweet clover patches at which they could nibble. There were fragrant woods in the valleys and, nearby, at the foot of a wispy willow tree, a sparkling creek chattered and rippled, gurgled and danced, and seemed to be laughing aloud. Maybe it laughed at its long queer name—for people called it Quequacommissicong Creek

—or maybe it laughed because it danced past such a very happy home just a few rods from where the two contented woodchucks lived.

Now a house so near the woodchucks' home might ordinarily have suggested danger, but not to these two. All the little wild things in the vicinity knew that no one who lived in this house had ever hurt a single living thing, for it belonged to a most tender-hearted family. Every one in this family loved not only children and beautiful scenery, but all the little wild creatures which ambled or flew, hopped or danced in the woods and fields.

In this house, surrounded by rolling lawns and trees and flowers and overlooking a beautiful garden, lived Wanda, Earle, Flavia, Howard—and Liesl, their cat. All of them were gentle and kind and thoughtful—even Liesl, who let the wrens build nests in the eaves of the porch and never worried them in the least.

All the little wild creatures were quite accustomed to the members of the family. The little brown field mice would sidle up to Wanda as she sat in her studio drawing pictures or writing stories for children. The birds, finding Howard and Earle at work in the garden, would hop closer and closer and cock their heads to look at them, or they would sing merrily from the tree tops nearby. The rabbits,

seeing Flavia studying insects, confidently hopped up to her, sat on their haunches and sniffed delicately to see what she was doing. Nothing really ran away from any member of the family and even the two plump contented woodchucks lumbered down the path knowing that they were perfectly safe.

Now during the year that the woodchucks first made their appearance, Pat and Janey came to visit Wanda and Earle and Flavia and Howard. Pat and Janey were twelve and ten and they came from Minnesota where Wanda and Howard and Flavia had lived when they were children. They loved to watch all the nosey little animals, so friendly and unafraid, but they simply shrieked with glee at the woodchucks as they had never seen woodchucks before. All day long they talked of them and imagined interesting things about them. They named one of them "Charles" (thinking it the proper nickname for "Chuck") and the other one "Pudgy" for that is just what the little rascal was—pudgy—*exceedingly* pudgy and plump and sleek and well-fed and very contented-looking. But alas! It did not take long to discover what made these two so chubby and round and hugeous! For Pudgy and Charles, not content with clover patches and crisp green shoots of meadow grass, liked to crawl through the garden fence and to eat the fresh, green vegetables, acting as though the garden were their very own.

Not only was the garden not theirs, but it was by no means an ordinary garden, for, although this tender-hearted family *ate* the vegetables in it, Wanda wanted more than anything else to *draw* it for the garden pictures she liked to make.

It had been planned with great care. The beans were planted beside long poles near the back of the garden so that they would not hide the vegetables at the front. They had also been planted toward the side so that the composition would be good. On the opposite side of the garden the tall stalks of sweet corn were placed so as to balance the beans, for Wanda, being an artist, would have felt unhappy if the garden had seemed to teeter toward the beans or to totter toward the corn.

All of the other vegetables were also planted so that Wanda could draw or paint the foliage in interesting patterns and colors. The light-colored lettuce stood next to the dark leaves of the chard. The feathery carrots looked lacy alongside of the stolid cabbages. Tomatoes were planted where red spots were most needed, and yellow crook-neck squashes lay picturesquely scattered about. It was a lovely garden indeed.

But Pudgy and Charles had no sense of the artistic. Now they ate the carrots, now the chard. They fairly mowed down the spinach and the delicate sprouts of the beets. And as for the beans—they ate them leaves, pods and all!

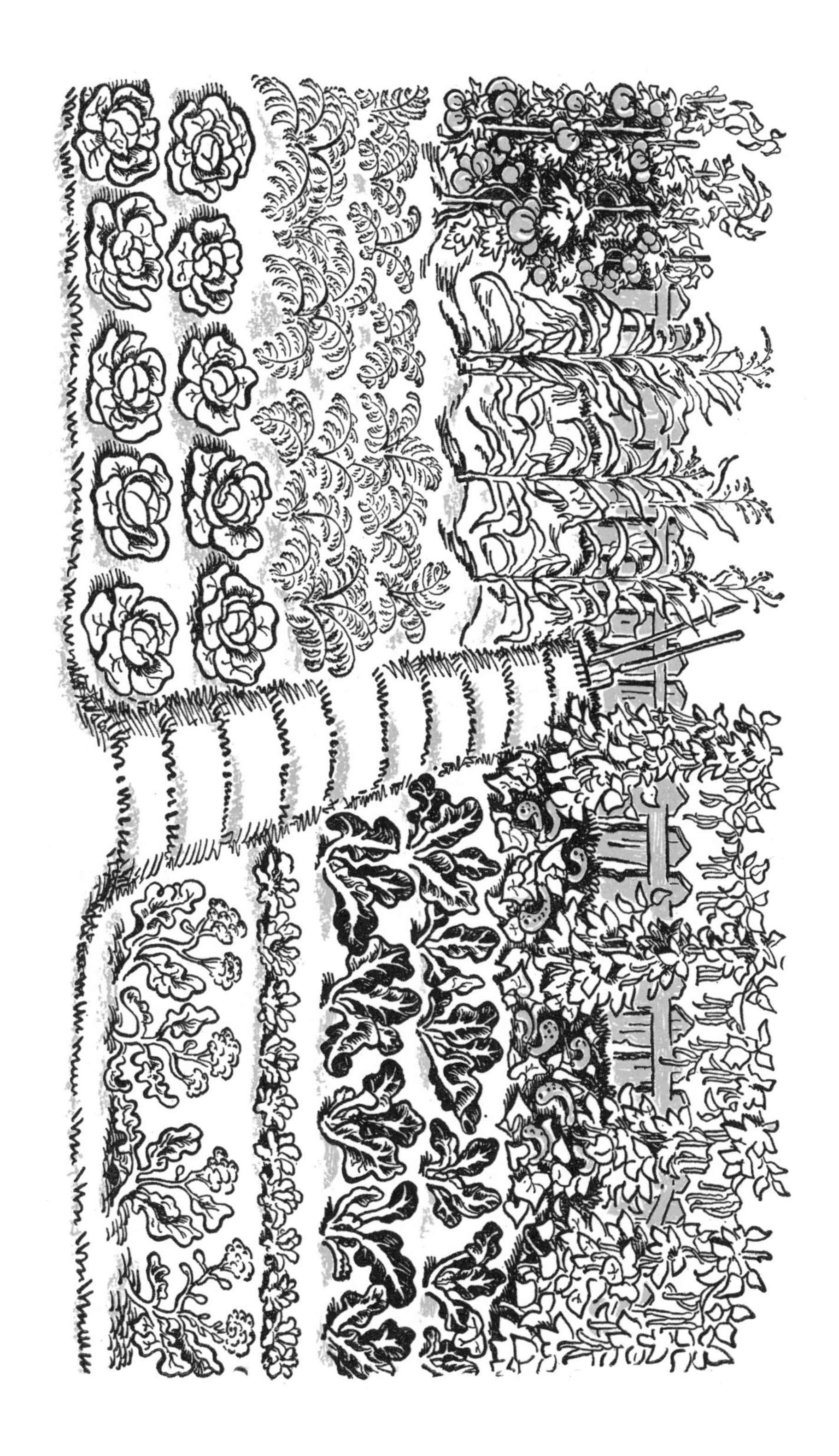

"Maybe," said Wanda, "we had better repair the fence. After all, the garden is very precious to us and Pudgy and Charles have all the great outdoors in which to find their salads!"

So Earle brought stout nails and boards and made the fence so solid that surely no little woodchuck could ever get through.

Pudgy and Charles, rascals that they were, gnawed through the newly repaired fence in a single night.

"If only they would eat *anything* but our beautiful garden," sighed Wanda.

"Maybe we should put up a wire fence," said Earle, and the rest of the family agreed. The next morning he and Howard drove twenty miles to town and twenty miles back and brought home some wire "strong enough to keep out little pigs."

"This will surely keep out Pudgy and Charles," they said with

conviction. All day long they hammered and pounded and pounded and hammered until they were very tired. By the time the sun was dropping behind the highest hill they had a good stout fence, with wire netting covering the pickets from top to bottom. But in the very dewiest early dawn Pudgy and Charles were unbelievably busy, and before the first rays of the morning sun shone pleasantly on the garden they had dug a gigantic hole under the new fence and feasted on the tender insides of seven heads of cabbage.

"What can we do now?" asked Wanda at the breakfast table.

"Maybe we could pile stones around the bottom of the fence so they can't dig," suggested Howard.

That sounded like a brilliant idea, so Howard and Earle carried the big, big stones and Wanda, Flavia, Pat and Janey filled in all the chinks with little ones. All day long they worked until by sun-

set they were very tired. Then, feeling well pleased with themselves, they sat down on comfortable lawn chairs to enjoy a well-earned rest. They leaned back contentedly, gloating over their accomplishment.

The first fireflies began to flit about cheerfully, the earliest stars twinkled pleasantly. All was serene and peaceful. Just at this point Pudgy and Charles appeared and quietly approached the garden path. Wanda and Earle, Howard, Flavia, Pat and Janey smiled smugly at one another. Let them come if they wished and they would find out who was the smarter in the end—people or woodchucks.

Pudgy and Charles tried to get through the fence, but it was no use. They tried to get under it, but the stones were so large and heavy that they could not dig their way through. They tried to gnaw, but the wire struck their teeth; and then, to the consternation of the assembled family, Pudgy and Charles calmly used the wire mesh as a ladder for their little black feet and climbed impudently right over the top!

Wanda watched aghast—what if they were to destroy the whole garden? What if the family had to drive twenty miles to get vegetables to eat? And besides, what crisp tid-bits would she have for the children who visited her, and *where* would she find a garden to draw?

For a long time she sat in the lawn chair and thought and thought. Finally, when everyone else but Flavia and Earle had gone to bed, she said: "I don't know what we can do about the garden. Pudgy and Charles don't seem to realize how important it is to us. They don't seem to be able to learn what we mean by our fences and things.

"It would be nice," she added as an after-thought, "if we could think of something with which we could sort of flavor the vegetables so that they wouldn't like them so well."

"Maybe they don't like pepper!" cried Flavia with enthusiasm and she ran to sprinkle some where she thought the woodchucks might reconnoiter the next day. But the pepper bothered them

little, and besides, the rain soon washed everything clean again.

The following day a neighbor dropped in to see the family and when he saw Pudgy and Charles and all the mischief they had done, he said: "You got to shoot the pesky things. Thick skin they have, hard head too—takes a big gun to kill them, but it's the only way."

Wanda and Earle looked at each other in horror and when the man left, Wanda whispered to Earle: "Do you think we would ever really have to do *that?*"

"It's a bad business," said Earle, "and maybe we should, but you know I need new glasses and I can't see to shoot very well and, as you know, little live things move and maybe I could never hit them and besides I haven't a gun. You know the man said it took a very special kind of gun, and the only gun I know of belongs to old Mr. Wigglesworth. We might be able to borrow that, but who knows how safe it is? It might even be in such bad shape that it would shoot backwards in which case it would be bad for us."

Wanda nodded her head in agreement. She was glad it hadn't been a good idea. But now Pudgy and Charles began to gnaw the fence posts and the front porch steps and the garage door, just to keep their teeth in trim for eating vegetables faster and better, it seemed.

"Tell you what we'll do," said Howard. "Every time we see them from now on we'll run after them and chase them just to show them that they mustn't chew up our garden and fence posts and

garage door and front porch steps. We must just teach them to live in their meadow."

When next Pudgy and Charles appeared, Howard and Earle started to chase them. Howard clapped his hands and yelled like

a fire siren as he ran, while Earle waved his arms like a windmill and roared in a deep gruff voice as he leaped over shrubs and flower beds in hot pursuit. Pudgy and Charles, startled by such unexpected commotion, scrambled in frenzied haste for their burrow. Their black feet twinkled in the sunshine as they ran, and Howard and Earle thought surely they were learning their lesson,

but as soon as they reached their burrow safely, Charles turned about and thrust out his nose as though chuckling defiantly at his pursuers.

The next day Wanda saw Pudgy and Charles swagger up to the broccoli. Sitting up on their hind legs they grasped the stems in their little black hands, and, pulling them down hand over hand until they could reach the tender heads, they devoured them with relish.

At this Wanda had a long talk with herself. She had never harmed anything in her life, but maybe, just maybe, these woodchucks were going a little too far. This time she conferred with Howard.

"What do you think, Howard? Things are getting pretty bad. Do you think, by any chance, maybe there would be a safe gun somewhere which wouldn't hurt Pudgy and Charles too much and yet scare them away somehow?"

Howard thought about the garden and the fence posts, the front porch steps and the garage door. "Perhaps I could borrow a gun from Mr. Boomer," said he, trying to be very firm, "but you know, Wanda, cartridges are very hard to get—maybe it would even take weeks and weeks to get the right size for the right kind of a gun."

"Well, Howard, maybe you misunderstood me a little," said Wanda, now quite overcome by this definite talk of guns and cartridges. "We mustn't do anything at all while Pat and Janey are here. They simply love the woodchucks and have endowed them with the most interesting personalities. To do anything *now* would be *unthinkable*."

"You are right, Wanda—definitely," said Howard, looking very much relieved, if the truth must be told. "There is plenty of time at some later date if things should really get bad."

And so Pudgy and Charles swashbuckled through the garden in freedom and safety as before.

At last there came a day when Pat and Janey had to go back to Minnesota. Now in ordinary families this might have been a

dangerous time for the woodchucks, but not for these two. If Flavia saw them saucily scurrying by she pretended to be very much absorbed in her insect book. If Howard saw them he quite suddenly remembered a light fixture which needed repairing. If Earle

saw them he felt a sudden need to tinker very busily with his car, or else he mowed the lawn energetically in the opposite direction from the woodchucks. And Wanda—well, Wanda kept right on drawing with *great* absorption.

Before long, Barbara Jean, the family's five-year-old niece, came on a visit. She laughed and squealed at the woodchucks just as Pat and Janey had done and, so once again, there was an excellent reason for not chasing them away.

And, of course, Charles and Pudgy were becoming simply ludicrously stout by this time. Their coats were stuffed to bursting and still they kept on eating the tomatoes, the ears of corn, the squashes and the muskmelons. In fact they ate only the very juiciest, ripest portions of many tomatoes, of numerous ears of corn, of countless squashes and dozens of muskmelons! They were really grossly greedy and roundly unreasonable.

After several weeks Barbara Jean left too.

Howard and Earle now held a conference. They felt convinced

—almost convinced at any rate—that, if the woodchucks were ever to be chased away, this might be the time to do it. So they approached Wanda with their plans.

"Yes, I know something should be done," said Wanda, "but you know, after all, it is late in the season and there is very little left in the garden which they can damage. The harvest is in and we did, somehow, after all, have enough for all of us to eat—and maybe they won't come back next year anyway."

"That's right," said Howard and Earle, "maybe they won't." Each rejoiced secretly that Wanda had had that happy thought!

Sure enough, by the time October was well begun, Charles and Pudgy were seen no more, and Wanda and Earle and Howard and Flavia packed up Liesl and moved back to New York for the winter. They thought that the problem had been neatly solved, indeed.

Meanwhile Pudgy and Charles slept peacefully in their burrow in the hillside, chuckling in their dreams perhaps, for never had they been better prepared to face the long winter's sleep. Many layers of plumpness, gathered from the kind-hearted family's garden, kept them warm and they slept on and on.

All winter long, while Pudgy and Charles slumbered peacefully, Wanda and Earle and Flavia and Howard worked busily in the

city, but late in April they decided that it was nearly time for them to move out to the country once more. Howard was the first to go and, as he approached the house, it looked sleepy from its long winter nap. The unkempt lawn, the locked workshop and the deserted-looking Guest House made him feel that he might be lonely over the week-end. But just at that moment, whom should he see

but Pudgy and Charles, with five plump babies trailing behind them. They were headed (alas yes!)—THEY WERE HEADED
DOWN
THE
GARDEN
PATH!